THE VIS

THE VISITOR

by

Hugh Studdert Kennedy

Introduction by
Adrian Plass

DARLEY ANDERSON
LONDON

First published in Great Britain
in 1934 by Putnam and Co Ltd.

This edition published in Great Britain
in 1990 by Darley Anderson, Estelle
House, 11 Eustace Road, London SW6 1JB

Printed and bound in Great Britain by
Courier International Ltd, Tiptree, Essex

ISBN 1 869838 20 3

Contents

Introduction by Adrian Plass   vii

A Foreword   ix

His First Coming   1

The Woodsman   8

The Record of Peter Darling   16

The Old Man at the Cave's Mouth   26

An Evening When He Did Not Come   34

The Tale of the City of Two Times Two   43

What Happened to John's Wife   54

To John's Wife

Introduction
by Adrian Plass

This rare and surprising book warms like a wood fire on a late autumn evening. Whimsy and wisdom flicker gently but illuminatingly through its pages, with an occasional sharp crack of revelation. I dislike almost all religious fiction, but here is one of the exceptions.

Hugh Studdert-Kennedy, brother of the famous Geoffrey known to many as "Woodbine Willie", had a gift that is uncommon in writers of all simple fiction, let alone the religious variety. Arthur Conan-Doyle was one of its greatest exponents using it to create the Sherlock Holmes legend. It is the gift of cosiness. Studdert-Kennedy makes us feel cosily welcome in the world of log cabin, forest path and simple people that provide the setting for encounters between the narrator—who could be you or I, or Studdert-Kennedy, or any warily curious human being—and the strange, arrestingly significant figure of the Visitor.

It would be too simple to describe this book as a series of parables, although the Visitor certainly uses the same technique of revealing truth through storytelling as the greatest exponent of the parable form; but there is more to it than that. It creates an almost magical atmosphere of hope and belief in a deeper, greater reality underlying and ultimately overcoming the negative aspects of life as we experience it.

The Visitor's radical insights and unsettling questions invite us, as we watch and listen from our privileged position as non-involved witnesses, to look afresh at old attitudes and patterns of thought. And it feels safe to do

Introduction

this in the company of the narrator, who unerringly questions and interjects just as most of us would do. Whether we agree with all of the writer's implied conclusions is another matter. Laying our dogma aside for a moment to hear what *The Visitor* has to say will be an entertaining and perhaps even a challenging experience.

I enjoyed it immensely.

A Foreword

IN Syria they have a story handed down through the centuries. It runs something like this:

Many thousands of years ago, Jesus and John the Baptist were on a journey together. And it came about that as they journeyed they passed through a desert place and in the heat of the day rested under the shadow of a great rock. All around them was nothing but desert, and so they waited, talking of the things of God till the sun went down, and then went their way.

Five thousand years later, Jesus and John the Baptist were passing that way again, and behold now, instead of the desert was a great city with gates on four sides of it and towers that reached to heaven. Being greatly astonished, they spoke to one of the citizens who stood near the gate at which they entered.

"Sir," they said, "we pray you tell us where is the great desert that once was here."

Whereat the man laughed, both he and his companions who stood by.

A Foreword

"A desert," he said, "why, friends, there has never been any desert hereabouts. Do you not know that this is The City, the great city, the days of which no man can tell, so many are they? And there is the great lake, and there the great rock in the midst of the lake, and, on top of the rock, you may see the great temple which the gods, I reckon, builded before the world was." And he laughed again and his friends also.

Five thousand years later, Jesus and John the Baptist were passing that way again; and, behold, now the great city was gone and in its place was a great forest. Only the lake was there, and in the midst of the lake, a great rock on the top of which the birds of the air made their nests. As they entered the forest they met a woodsman and thus addressed him:

"Sir," they said, "tell us what has become of the great city that once was here."

"A great city," said the woodsman. "Now, what a strange question is that, for indeed, sirs, hereabouts has never been a great city, but only this great forest. Here have I laboured, and my father and his father before him, in the great

A Foreword

forest by the great lake with the great rock in the midst of the lake on which the birds of the air have always made their nests." And he went his way.

And so it came about that another five thousand years went by, and, once again, Jesus and John the Baptist were passing that way, and, behold, now the forest was gone and all around them was nothing but desert, as it had been in the beginning, and, in the midst of the desert, a great rock. And there was no man to ask concerning the matter, so they rested under the shadow of the rock and talked of the things of God.

There is a path whicn no fowl knoweth,
and which the vulture's eye hath not seen.

JOB

CHAPTER ONE

His First Coming

WHY did he come to me? I do not know unless it was that he knew I would know him, or at any rate hoped that I would, and determined to take a chance on it. I had never seen him before. And yet, when I opened my cabin door, on that late autumn evening when he first came, and saw him standing in the half light, a calm silhouette against a calm sky, I held out my hand to him in eager welcome.

A few minutes later, he was sitting in the other chair at the other side of the fire holding out his hands to the blaze.

What a strange man he was! Strange because to this day I cannot describe him. Was he gracious? Was he handsome? Was he kind? Was he graceful in movement, beautiful of voice? How old was he? What was the manner of his dress and degree? I do not know. I only know that whatever at any time was the response in me to the appeal of beauty and grace and kindliness, that was always

The Visitor

present when he was by. All the beauty of the ages of man and woman he seemed to bear about with him.

He never told me where he came from. I never asked him. I never connected him with the idea of going and coming. He acquired a way, after a time, of coming in quietly unannounced, especially towards dusk, when the only light in my cabin came from the little lamp on my desk and the fitful glow of a log fire. I would look up and see him sitting calmly and all serene in the other chair. I might not have seen him for days and weeks, but he always acted as though he had never gone away and as though the last time I had seen him was but a few moments before. I got into the way of calling him, and thinking of him as the Visitor.

He always had a specific reason for coming. The first time, for instance, he quickly made known his quest. I had excused myself, as I would do to an old friend; had asked him to make himself comfortable before the fire while I completed some work at my desk which had to be cleared out of the way. As soon as I had finished, he spoke.

His First Coming

"I wanted to ask you," he said, "about fear."

"Yes?" I said inquiringly. "What about it? There does seem to be a lot of it everywhere— everywhere one turns. The man who has not is afraid he never will have. The man who has is afraid he will lose what he has. What do you make of it?"

He laughed softly, as one might who knew exactly what he wanted to say, but was, for the moment, uncertain as to how. "Have you ever," he said at length, "tried to get a hen out of a wire enclosure? You are thinking only of the hen's best interests. You are not an enemy, but a friend. No injury whatever is threatening her, In the place to which you would guide her there are food and drink in abundance the things that she greatly desires, yet, through some misunderstanding, what ought to be a gracious, orderly procedure is being transformed under your eyes into a tragedy. She throws herself in an agony of protest against the wire; she dives into it. Two or three doors are open wide; she ignores them, runs past them and hurls herself anew on another stretch of wire. She is not only perfectly free to escape from any danger that may seem to threaten, but there is no danger threatening. She is and ought to be at peace with the world, and yet there is all this turmoil."

He paused and looked into the fire with that kindly universal interest I seemed always to have known. I did not speak. I felt that he was working his way through to some new vantage ground. After a little while he continued as though speaking to himself.

"Curious, isn't it? It is just the same with the world, with men and women. To anyone who sees things as they really are it must appear at first so incomprehensible."

Again I waited, and in a few moments he took up his parable.

"For years," he said, "I tried to find out the cause of all the turmoil, but I came to see long ago that it all comes from the fear of and belief in death. I wonder what you think of it. If we were sure that we were not going to die, or that our friends were not going to die, how many troubles would be shorn of half their agony; how many would disappear over night! Think of it.

His First Coming

"As I came along just now, for instance, up the road which leads to the four corners—you know, the one from which you get the best view of the lake—I saw a young girl standing at her garden gate looking anxiously up and down the road. I had often seen her there before and spoken to her—we are old friends. But then of course you know her. She is John's wife." I nodded assent, and he went on—"She is, as you know, married but a few months and happy as the day is long. But, this evening, there was no happiness in her face, only—only trouble.

"I asked her about it.

" 'Oh, sir,' she said, 'it is John; he is over an hour late and he has never been late before and I cannot think of anything that could be keeping him.'

" 'Well,' I said, 'what are you afraid of?'

" 'Oh, I am afraid that something may have happened to him.'

" 'What kind of a something, child?'

" 'He may have been hurt somehow.'

" 'And if you knew that he had been hurt, what would you fear then?'

[5]

The Visitor

"But I did not wait for an answer. Her expression was enough. I hastened to tell her— I ought to have done it sooner perhaps, but I wanted her to see this thing—I hastened to tell her that she need not worry because I had seen and spoken with John in the village below. I told her how glad and joyful I had found him because—and this was the cause of the delay— because some splendid new work had come his way. He was, I told her, torn between a desire to go and clinch the matter, as he felt he ought to do, and to run all the way home to tell her, as he most desired to do. He would be coming soon.

"In a moment, all fear and anxiety were gone, and only joy remained. So I asked her, 'Tell me, child, if in the midst of all your fear someone, whom you knew was always right, had told you that your husband could not be dead, would you have been as afraid as you were?'

"She thought a moment. 'Why, no,' she said, 'I know I would not. I never thought of it, but if death were out of the way I do not think that I would ever be afraid of anything again, for I would always have John.'

His First Coming

"Isn't it strange?" he said, slowly, after another pause, " 'I would always have John.' So humble —so unutterably grateful for crumbs—so fearful they will be denied us."

And then, as though he had entirely forgotten my presence, "Isn't it strange, when the whole table is spread for the feast—and we are all bidden —everyone?"

CHAPTER TWO

The Woodsman, and What Came of It

WHAT did he mean by it? In a vague way I guessed. I am not at all a visionary. Indeed I have always prided myself—secretly—on an abundant common sense. Still I have never been able to shake myself free from the uncomfortable feeling that someone somewhere, who sees things as they really are, is laughing at us. Or, rather, when I take myself to task on the matter, I have an uncomfortable feeling that if any one of us could see himself and his surroundings, his aims and his achievements, as they really are, he would laugh at himself.

This evening as I climbed up the hill to my cabin the thought was strong upon me. That illustration of his about the hen bothered me. There it seemed to be so remorselessly in a nutshell—the two worlds, the hen's world as seen from within, filled at that moment so full of fear and threatening and disaster only to be averted by frantic effort; and the hen's world

The Woodsman

as seen from without pervaded only by comfort and protection and a desire to help. And then the young wife. Of course the world smiled at her seeing so much in John. I knew John. He was an ordinary enough kind of fellow, decent enough, energetic enough, but cast in much the same mould as millions of others. And yet to the young wife he was everything. Well, that had been the way from the beginning.

"She will get over it," I said to myself, half aloud, as I stood looking out from my west window to where the sun was just going down in a blaze of glory behind a skyline of spruce. "She will get over it. Two years from now she may count herself lucky if she sees John as I see him."

Somehow, the thought saddened me, and I was about to turn away with a gesture of impatience when my attention was arrested by a familiar voice. It was the Visitor. He had come in so quietly that I had not heard him and was already seated in the other chair resting easily as if he had been there for some time.

"But why should she?" he said. His question was my question of course.

The Visitor

"Have you ever stopped to ask yourself," he continued, "if it might not be possible that she is seeing John rightly now; that she is the only one who has ever seen John rightly; and that if she loses her vision in a year or two and sees him as you see him, she will be seeing him wrongly?" He got up and walked to the door with the freedom of an old friend and opened it, letting in a flood of red sunlight, and then, returning to his seat, went on, as if his action had suggested a new line of thought.

"It is curious how we accept the opening and closing theory of life, isn't it? The good and the evil; how firmly convinced we are that good is too good to be true; how prone we are to insist that the highest and the best, the most satisfying and the most welcome, must necessarily be in the realm of illusion!

"Look at John. You see him as an ordinary workman, as you call him, living a very ordinary life, following a very ordinary course, moved by very ordinary hopes and desires. She sees him as some radiant thing. The sound of his voice brings joy to her heart. She loves everything connected with him. The sight of his coat thrown aside on the kitchen chair reminds her of how much she loves him, how good and great and splendid he is and how he does all things well. You are inclined to laugh at her, but how do you know that it may not be that her eyes are opened where yours are closed and that, looking up instead of down, she is seeing the angel? Has it ever occurred to you to wonder what this world would be like if we could all always see each other as this girl sees John? And do you not think it might be possible that we would all be much nearer right if we did?"

He stopped speaking and my eyes wandered out of the window to where the path wound downwards, a thin brown ribbon, through the trees to the valley. Some little way along the path I caught sight of the bent figure of an old woodsman whom I knew well, returning to his cabin for the night. He was a very plain old man, yet it suddenly came to me that he had a life behind him and around him of which I knew nothing. For seventy years and more he had been living and thinking, hoping, building

The Visitor

castles in the air, rising in the morning full of joy, or going to bed sorrowful. What did I know of him and wherewith did I judge him? And yet if I had been asked I would have said I knew him well. Was there someone somewhere who saw him as the young wife saw John, and if so which one of us was right?

I was interrupted by the Visitor's voice. It came to me as the summing up of my own thought.

"Yes," he said quietly, "is it not just so? What *do* you know about him? But supposing I could take you to some vantage point whence you could see him as he really is, pass through the labyrinth of his life as it has been and as he has passed through it, see his struggles as he has seen them, shrink with him under the lash of unkindness, weep tears with him under the benediction of love, watch with him through the hours of hope deferred, brace up with him in the hour of new resolve, stand by with him in the hour of patient drudgery, stay with him as he watches the years pass, pray with him in the hour of separation, lift up your heart with

The Woodsman

him as he goes on his way home, down hill now, all the way, hoping in his patient old heart that at even-tide there may be light—what then?"

By this time the old woodsman had disappeared round the bend in the road, walking straight on, so it seemed to me, into the glory of a golden sky.

"It is strange," I said, half aloud, "but he already seems different. I do not know anything about his life, but he must have passed through all those experiences and in every one of them my heart goes out to him. Already he is more to me than ever before, a very noble gentleman. I feel somehow as if I wanted to beg his pardon, to take the shoes from off my feet because the place whereon I am standing is—holy ground."

The Visitor smiled. "Yes, it is holy," he said quietly, "it is always holy, and, as we set ourselves to see it so, it will be so indeed, for so it is in truth."

And then suddenly he laughed that wonderful, joy inspiring laugh of his, and, reaching out to a little shelf of books close at hand, picked up a well-worn copy of Dickens' "Christmas Carol."

The Visitor

"You remember," he said, "the place where Scrooge wakes up from the dream and is so glad to find that he is alive, and that there is yet time to do good and to see people as they really are? How he rushes to the window and flings it wide open and takes deep breaths of the clear, sparkling morning air, listens to the Christmas bells, hails a passing boy and sends round to the corner grocer's for the prize turkey and sends the prize turkey to Bob Cratchit? And then, you remember, how after a shave and a careful dressing up in honour of the day, he fares forth, all in his best, into the streets, into a world transformed, walks along with his hands behind him regarding everyone with a delighted smile, and how he looks so 'irresistibly pleasant' that 'three or four good humoured fellows' say, 'Good morning, Sir! A Merry Christmas.'

"But listen: 'He went to church, and walked about the streets and watched the people hurrying to and fro, and patted children on the head, and questioned beggars and looked down into the kitchens of houses, and up at the windows, and found that everything could yield him

The Woodsman

pleasure. He never dreamed that any walk—that anything—could give him so much happiness'."

As the Visitor was reading the concluding sentences he seemed to forget me again. He read very softly and very slowly, as if visualizing each picture as it was conjured up, the children, the beggars, the kitchens, the windows and the joy of it all.

As he closed the book I heard him repeating to himself, "'He never dreamed that any walk—that anything—could give him so much happiness.' I wonder if Dickens really understood. I sometimes think he did."

CHAPTER THREE

The Record of Peter Darling

IT was some weeks before I saw the Visitor again. However, I did not expect him sooner. "He will come," I said to myself, "when I have sorted out this stuff he has left me, but not until then. That idea of his about Scrooge and the woodsman and the young wife and John—it would be interesting to try it out."

And so I set about it.

But, almost immediately, I was confronted with a difficulty. I found that sometimes it was easy and sometimes utterly impossible to see people any differently from the way I had always seen them. So much seemed to depend upon how I felt, what mood I was in, how I was faring, what I had been reading; upon a thousand things. At other times, the whole idea seemed just foolish. All the "plain Jane and no nonsense" in me was up in arms, and "seeing is believing" seemed to be enthroned.

At other times again—and I marvelled at

the eagerness with which I welcomed their advent—the way that the Visitor pointed out seemed to be the only possible way. Such times, however, were few and far between. For the most part I was beset with doubt. At first, I had stepped forth with abounding faith; this idea of the Visitor's was a sure key that would unlock all manner of mysteries; it would succeed every time. But it did not, and the more frequently I failed the more attention and credence did I give to the arguments against its verity which assailed me from every side.

I remembered with some bitterness a remark once made to me by a famous writer, now long dead, that so much of the effectiveness of any writing depended upon the reader's mood. Young and full of faith at the time, I had repudiated such an idea with a laugh; but it had come back to me again and again since. Who was right, Philip drunk or Philip sober? Philip in his early cups with all the world aglow, or Philip the morning after the night before, with all the world grey and all life aimless? And, in between these extremes, what was the moment

The Visitor

of right seeing? Which was right, the man on his way to work, with bright and shining morning face, or the man on his way back home again with an Ishmaelitish day behind him? Why was there so much morning and evening? How humiliating it was, this cloud of emotion, expectant, fulfilled or thwarted, which swayed me this way and that, and really influenced me so much more than I knew, even when I thought I was being most detached!

"What difference does it make, how you become an optimist?" I muttered to myself as I got up from under a great pine tree where I had been lying in the half-shade, and took the back road home. "Some men are born drunk, some achieve drunkenness, and some have drunkenness thrust upon them." I laughed rather grimly, as I walked along under the trees, and then was silent.

There was a rustle of fallen leaves on the path behind me and I looked round. It was the Visitor. I waited for him gladly. The next moment he had caught up with me. A word of greeting and we were walking on together—

Peter Darling

in silence, both enjoying the fresh cool air which came up from the valley already in the shadow.

"You know," he said after a time, "you are wrong. It isn't really a matter of chance."

"How do you mean?" I asked.

"Well," he said, "curiously enough, just before I came up with you I was recalling what you might call a case in point. You remember old Mrs. Darling who used to live in the little cottage by the railway crossing, near the creek; or was she before your time?"

"No, I remember her very well. She had the most wonderful ducks, hadn't she? White ducks, the whitest I ever saw. She used to wash each one separately every Saturday evening. Mother Darling, the children called her. Yes, indeed, I remember her well. What of her?"

"Well, if you remember her, you will remember Peter Darling, the son."

"Yes, I remember him, too. A tall, good-looking chap. Disappeared suddenly and no one ever seems to have known what became of him."

"The story is about Peter," said the Visitor,

The Visitor

"I have always known all about it. He was, you know, 'the only son of his mother, and she was a widow' "—it was a way the Visitor had, quite naturally, of just using the words of the Bible whenever they fitted his purpose—"and they were everything to each other; where she went he went and where he went she went—until the lad was sixteen or seventeen. And then, one summer evening, the mother came home, and found the door open and a note on the table. It was from Peter, a very cruel note, telling her bluntly he was going away, that she need not try to look for him, and that he had taken the money from the jar on the mantelpiece which she had saved against his going to college in the autumn. It was his, he said, anyway, and he would use it as he wanted to.

"He never came back. I used to go in to see her often. She was hurt as only a mother can be hurt by such a blow, but never for a moment did it shake her faith in her boy. It was not that she forgave him, but that she seemed to think that there was nothing to forgive. The real Peter had no more to do with taking that money and going away than the sun had to do with the world's night.

" 'Peter is all right,' she said to me one day, 'and I guess all the world is all right—really. And we will see that some day when we stop chasing shadows. Play acting doesn't scare me. I know it's all "dress up." And most of people's bad doings are play acting.'

"And so she went on through the years. A few weeks before she died, she handed me a letter she had written to Peter, and asked me to give it to him if ever I should see him again. She felt sure that I would."

"And did you?" I ventured after a moment; for he had stopped speaking and seemed suddenly to be miles away yet instantly within hail. I know no better way to describe it. He did not reply at once, but, after a little while, looked at me with that sudden reassuring smile of his, and went on with his story.

"Oh, yes," he said, "I found him several years afterwards, in a great city, many miles from here. He was coming out of a billiard-room with the word 'waster' written all over him. I

The Visitor

handed him his mother's letter, and he read it as we stood together under a street light. I never saw what was in that letter. Mother Darling had left it unsealed, but I never felt, somehow, that I was free to read it. Whatever it was, it worked a miracle. Peter said nothing for a moment or two. He just stood and looked straight in front of him. But as he stood, his face seemed to change, to clear somehow, as if something had suddenly been wiped out and away. His figure seemed to straighten up and fill out.

" 'How long,' he asked at last, 'has she been thinking like this?' holding out the letter to me.

" 'I have never read the letter, Peter,' I said, 'but I do know this, that she never once thought of you save as the boy she had always known and loved. She never thought of you as of someone who had gone wrong and would some day go right again, but as someone whose real self had never really gone wrong. She never said, "Peter *will* be all right." It was always, "Peter *is* all right." '

"He was silent for a moment, and then turning

Peter Darling

to me asked quietly, 'And what do you think?'

" 'I think the same as your mother, Peter. I think you are all right.'

" 'Then I guess I must be.'

"There was another pause, and then, 'I guess the first thing is to get a job.'

" 'Yes,' I said, 'I think that would be the first thing.'

"He slowly squared his shoulders, looked up the street and down it again and then—

" 'I know a man who will give me a job. Good-bye and thank you. I will write.'

" 'Yes, do,' I said, 'good-bye.'

"The next moment he had turned the corner and was gone. That was several years ago. This morning I had my first letter from him. He has made good and more than good. You shall read the whole letter, but here is one sentence which seems to me to sum up all the others —listen. 'I quickly learned that my mother was right, that there is only one way to remedy a mistake, and that is to see it as a mistake about something that is true, and then determine to see what is true and only that.

[23]

The Visitor

Everything wrong, whether it is in what happens to us or what people do to us, is a mistake about something right. I cannot explain myself better than that, but somehow it works when I see things that way. You can't hate people when you know that, if only their eyes were open to their mistake, they would be on your side every time, and all the time.' "

We walked on together in silence. Inwardly, for some reason or other, I felt goaded by irritation. All this did not solve my problem, did not even touch upon it. Some people were born that way, some people just stumbled on to it; but how to find the way, and walk in it, and enjoy in it that supreme naturalness without which all life becomes a pose, that was the question.

"Oh, yes, it can be done." The Visitor's voice came to me with its usual assuring calm. "It can be done because it has to be done. Nothing really happens by chance. The moment we think about it we know that to be true and must be true. Mother Darling came to understand a great truth, and she found a way of presenting

Peter Darling

it which would enable Peter to see it too, and the moment Peter really saw it, that moment it became—I suppose the scientists would call it dynamic. In other words, it worked. The great question is how did Mother Darling learn it, and how did Peter come to see it?"

We had reached a point in the road where an opening in the pine trees revealed a great vista of the valley beneath, and the mountains beyond. We both paused as a matter of course.

"I think they understood," said the Visitor after a moment, "because they caught a sudden glimpse of life, such as we are catching of that valley. They saw everything, suddenly, in a just proportion. It is all a matter of looking and walking in the right direction, and some people never find the right path until they have bruised their feet on all the wrong ones. But let us talk of it more when we get indoors. You know the old saying, 'Man's extremity is God's opportunity.' Like many another old saying, it is true enough."

CHAPTER FOUR

The Old Man at the Cave's Mouth

THE wind had risen, blowing in from the ocean great clouds of rain which whipped against the windows, and fell from the eaves in a steady drip. Without, was all storm. Within, was a blazing fire and that strange sense of detachment which only such a haven in the midst of tempest can bring. The Visitor was seated in his chair spreading out his hands to the flames.

"It is a good setting for a talk," he said with a smile. "Do you want to talk?"

I assented eagerly. After a moment he went on, following, as he always did, an unexpected course.

"I have often wondered, as you know," he said, "what we would think of it if we could really see life as it is; if we could see it for what it really must be, a succession of mental experiences expressed in this curiously cumbersome style which we call material.

"Take the case of the man whose steps seem

The Old Man

to be dogged with misfortune. To him, and to those around him, it seems as if *things* always grouped themselves in the wrong way for him. Yet what is it that really must be happening to him? Must it not be that this thing called misfortune—this mistake as to adjustment—is expressing itself to him in a hundred different ways? The *effect* is always the same, almost humdrum in its sameness; the same sense of being baffled, hounded; the bewildered conviction that there ought to be someone somewhere to whom one should be able to go and *protest*, and have the thing righted; the same sense of grievance; the same wretched misery; the same age-old complaint, 'If only I could have done this or that, or known in time not to do thus and so'; the same smouldering wretchedness at seeing the world go by and go on just as if nothing had happened. No matter what *shape* misfortune takes, it can only affect us, if we allow ourselves to be affected by it, in these ways. The process is all mental, of course, all centred in our own thought, as we see quite clearly the moment we begin to combat it.

The Visitor

"I remember, years ago, in a little village thousands of miles away from here, there lived an old woman. She used to come for scraps—anything one had left over. She had had what the world would call a hard life, and it continued to be hard right to the end. Yet I always felt she was happy, and for this reason: the moment an evil was presented to her she immediately sought, not for patience or resignation to bear it, but for a compensation with which, as it were, to neutralize its effect upon her. She always found it. If in passing her on the road, for instance, I remarked to her that it was a wet night, she would reply, 'Yes, but it is good for the roots'; or if I remarked that it was a cold night, she would reply, 'Yes, but it is dry under foot.' One day her little lean-to shed in which she kept her tools and seeds and other things for her garden was burned down. I went round to commiserate, but found her too happy to speak for thankfulness that it was not her *house*.

"Don't you see what a mental thing it is, the *misery* of misfortune met and routed by the joy

The Old Man

of gratitude, and that without any change in *things*? It is such an old, old story, of course, but nobody knows it. The triumph of good over evil has been the theme of the story teller since the beginning of time. The happy ending is more than ever the demand of the hour, but nobody really knows anything about it. Why? Because everybody always thinks of it as expressed in terms of *things*. The happy ending, or rather the *happiness* which is at last enthroned, is a mental and spiritual condition, and yet the world believes that it can only be brought about by the rearrangement of material things."

He looked at me and laughed; laughed, I suppose, because my whole attitude must have reflected the curious turmoil that was going on within; every now and again a ray of light, then clouds and clouds and clouds; anon a blaze of glory, the last ascent to the mountain top, the Horeb height where all is revealed; and then the clouds again. What did he really mean? I wondered if I saw, if I caught even a glimpse.

The Visitor

He leaned towards me for a moment with an inexpressible gesture of kindliness, and then, settling quietly back again, looked into the fire. We were both silent, listening to the wind as it whistled through the eaves, and to the rain as it splashed in great scuds against the window panes. Gradually, a sense of peace came over me, and, next moment, the Visitor was speaking.

"Look at it this way," he said. "The storm without at this moment sounds wild and cruel, but we know that it will vanish away; the sun has set some hours, but we know that it will rise again; the winter will soon be here, but we know that after the winter will be the spring and the summer. None of these things moves us or invades our peace. In the infinite realm of eternal order and harmony, for ever undisturbed, these things count for nothing. If our happiness, our sense of harmony, our rest in the midst of seeming restlessness is there founded, storm or fair weather, cloud or clear sky, are of no moment. If they appear, it is only to disappear in the presence of an all-embracing consciousness of peace.

The Old Man

"When, by so thinking, we conquer a momentary sense of fear or sorrow and our serenity returns to us, all that has really taken place, surely, is the exchange of one mental condition for another. The world insists that this exchange can only be brought about by a rearrangement of circumstances, and as long as the world so believes, it will have to be brought about in that way. But there is another way. It is the way of the old woman who came for the scraps. Somewhere in the depths of her genial old soul she caught a glimpse of the fact that happiness is not a product of circumstances, but *a great fact of life*, for time and eternity, and that, to the man who understands this fact, circumstances can neither give anything nor take anything away."

As he spoke, the storm seemed to rise to a greater fury than ever before as if in protest against such doctrines. The wind swirled through the tree tops, whipping wet leaves against the window which looked towards the ocean and echoing on up the mountain side. The Visitor's voice grew fainter.

The Visitor

Then, suddenly, I ceased to hear it altogether, and I had travelled back years of time and was sitting on a small stool opposite a brightly glowing fire, and a beautiful voice was reading to me. I was conscious of an eager interest and a great expectation, for we were reaching the climax of a wonderful story—about an old man who having climbed up a steep hillside was standing at the mouth of a cave, looking out into a storm of wind and rain. He had fled there from his enemies. He was old and weary and disappointed, and many of his friends had been slain before his eyes. Indeed, he was the only one left, and his enemies sought him in order that they might take him and kill him too. But as he stood in the mouth of the cave—the beautiful voice read on—a strange thing happened to him. He suddenly saw that in all this trouble which seemed to encompass him on every side there could not be anything of truth.

The storm broke in all its fury, yet he did not retreat but stood at the cave's mouth. And first there came a great wind, but he saw clearly that God was not in the wind; and then a great

The Old Man

earthquake, but God was not in the earthquake; and after the earthquake a fire, but God was not in the fire; and after the fire "a still small voice."

And this still, small voice became the voice of the Visitor, as out of a great distance I seemed to hear him saying again: "Happiness is not a product of circumstances, but a great fact of life, for time and eternity, and to the man who understands this fact circumstances can neither give anything nor take anything away."

CHAPTER FIVE

An Evening When He Did Not Come

I HAD been away all day in the great city, the city whose million lights illumined the night sky as seen from my cabin door away to the south, and the sputter and the roar and the "thou shalt not" of it had seemed more pronounced than ever before.

I am very far from being a reactionary. Dreams of a possible return to a golden age have no attraction for me. The great city and all that it means stir deeps of interest within me seldom otherwise plumbed. Nevertheless, every now and again, in the midst of it, when invention and progress and civilization seem most triumphant, there will descend upon me a sudden fearful realization that to anyone a few miles up in the air the city would be a speck, and no man could be seen therein.

The stillness of the countryside seemed especially grateful as the little train left me at my wayside station, and wound its way with much

He Did Not Come

echoing and re-echoing of effort further on among the hills. Before taking the winding path up the hillside I paused to listen, waiting eagerly for the small sounds of hedgerow and spinney to resume possession after the energetic puffing of the little engine had faded away in the distance. It was not long. The faint drone of a stag-beetle's wings close at hand, a few moments later, told me that the unseen choir had the floor without dispute once again.

"Well, it is good to be back," I said to myself as I mounted the hill, well content.

And yet—that evening, when the firelight danced on the walls and the lamp had been lit, and, with my papers spread out on my desk, I was about to set to work, I knew I was not so well content after all. In the great city, as I was leaving, I had bought an evening paper. I had forgotten about it in the train, but now, as it came to my hand, I opened it out, intending to glance through it, and read it more at my leisure later on. I was attracted, however, by an article on an inside page, and, after reading the first few sentences, continued on to the end.

The Visitor

It was by a young newspaper man from a foreign country, a fresh, engaging boy—for his photograph was there—who looked out at me with a tremendous interest from behind a pair of horn-rimmed spectacles. He had joined the staff of the paper on a kind of exchange basis, and, after he had been in that great city for a time, he would go on to another great city and so write his way hither and yon and finally home.

He had just arrived. All agog with interest and all beset with dreams, he told of his journey up the coast. He wrote of the azure sky and the golden mists and the wonderful headlands and the white breakers on the edge of a blue sea. Then he spoke of some islands he had seen, three of them—I knew them well—rising up suddenly out of the waters, and of how he had always loved an island, and always dreamed of how one day he would surely own one, and build his own house and till his own fields, and go out in the early morning, as all true islanders should, with his fowling piece to find what he might.

He Did Not Come

And as I read, before I knew it, I had travelled back some twenty-five years or more and had taken his place. Suddenly it was I who was writing, I who was casting round for a word, I who was dreaming dreams and seeing visions and struggling to get them out on paper.

It was I who paused every now and again to read what I regarded as an exceptionally fine passage and I who was filled with thoughts of how this person would read it and that person would read it, and how this man would ask his neighbour if he had read it, and how my editor would surely mark me as one who had a great future. And it was I, too, who suddenly did not care whether any of these things happened if only I could write so as to tell others of all the wonderful things I saw.

And so on—and on.

As I came to myself, my eyes travelled across the room to a corner where a pile of old books spread out in strange disarray caught the fitful glow of the firelight. They represented the contents of a sack full of ancient volumes with strange title pages and crumbling calf bindings

The Visitor

which I had bought some time before for a small sum at a country auction. Some of them had proved to be treasures. Most of them had proved to be of no value. All of them had appealed to me as interesting in a way all their own.

But now, as I surveyed them, there descended upon me a strange sense of weariness. Thousands of miles away from where I sat, ten score years back in time, a little more, maybe a little less, the writers of these books were busying themselves about their great task. With what high thoughts was this one filled as he went about his business, with what satisfaction did he make him a new pen and set about it; or, with what sense of inadequacy or foiled purpose did he lay the pen down again some morning as a courier passed his open window in a cloud of dust on his way to town; some evening as the wains creaked homewards from the hayfields; some night as the voice of the watchman cried to the silence all around that it was a fine night and all was well!

How they had all travailed and rejoiced, lifted up their hearts to the heights or been cast

He Did Not Come

down into the deeps. How had this one been
puffed up; how had that one trifled along; how
had this worthy minister of the gospel girded
himself anew every morning for the fray; how
had this graceful dabbler in Belles Lettres written
an ode to his mistress' eyebrow or conceived a
merry quip about Master So-and-So.

What a business it had all been, to be sure!
What long labour with quill and tablet, what
reading and re-reading, what journeyings on
horseback to and from the printer, what music
in the creaking and groaning of the wooden
presses, what binding and lettering and polishing!
And then, at last, the day when that copy over
here in the corner, that same book, with its
brown calf covers and its title in red and gold,
now dusty and worn but then all resplendent,
was sold for the first time to some gentleman
of discernment, and thus set out on its long
journey down the years.

What was to be made of it all? There was
that boy, away in the great city, writing as if no
one had ever written before, all hailing the
sunrise as a new wonder and the sunset as

The Visitor

something concerning which the world stood in sad
need of being informed. And there were the
writers "dead and gone" whose joys and sorrows
and leaping up of heart might still be seen and
felt through those musty pages.

And here was I, a traveller in the middle
way, still eager, if it might be so given to me,
to mount with the wings of an eagle, still eager
to run and not be weary, still praying when the
way seemed dark that I might be able to "walk
and not faint."

What did it all amount to and what was it all
about?

I looked up. He ought to have been there.
I needed him. But the other chair was empty,
and the door was closed, and the pile of old
books in the corner seemed as I watched them
to fade away slowly into the shadow.

"I guess he is not coming," I said, laughing
suddenly at the completeness with which the
reverie had taken hold of me. "This will never
do; I must get to work."

Mechanically I began to set my papers in
order, and as I did so I uncovered a note which

He Did Not Come

I must have overlooked when I first came in. It was addressed to myself, and I recognized at once the happy, half-formed hand of John's wife. It was just a little note thanking me for some small service I had done her. But there was a postscript—longer than the letter—in which she told me that, just as she was finishing, our friend had come in, and upon her telling him that she was writing to me he had asked her to include a message from himself.

"I do not know what it means, of course," she wrote—and I could hear her laughing happily—"but he asks me to tell you that he thinks you will find what you want on the fly-leaf of the old Bible you were showing him the other day."

With a strange new feeling of interest I laid down the note, and taking a candle from my desk went towards the corner, now it seemed almost completely in darkness, where the old books had come to rest. Next moment I had found the Bible and had opened at the fly-leaf eager to read what was written. There were just two lines, in brown and faded ink and the

The Visitor

strange pointed handwriting of a century and
more ago. At first, it seemed as if it would be
almost impossible to decipher, so faded was it,
but at last there emerged clearly these words,
"Without father, without mother, without de-
scent, having neither beginning of days nor end
of life."

Slowly I came back to my desk and sat down.
What did it mean? I seemed to be a long time
before I got an answer. At last it came to me,
and lo! the old writers had ceased to be old and
the young writer had ceased to be young and
I had ceased to stand in the middle way and we
were all of the same age. And there was no
birth and no death, no maturity and no decay,
only the continued for ever unfoldment of infinite
being.

Lifting my head from my hands, I looked
towards the other chair. It was still empty, but
the room seemed to be filled with a much-loved
presence.

CHAPTER SIX

The Tale of the City of Two Times Two

"I WONDER," he said, "did you ever hear the story of the City of Two Times Two?" It was the Visitor who spoke. He had come upon me suddenly late one evening as I sat on the great rock overlooking the valley, not far away from my cabin door. The moon was rising grandly above the distant tree-tops, a globe of shining mottled gold inconceivably huge and resplendent. I was marvelling at the silence and peace which seemed to pervade the whole world. Now and again, some distance down the hill, a tree-toad would lift up his voice and then stop suddenly as if to make sure that all was safe. When he was still, there was no sound anywhere.

It was in one of these intervals that I saw him coming towards me through the moonlight, his tall, spare form throwing a long shadow before him.

"I looked for you in your room," he said as

The Visitor

he held out his hand with that gracious hesitancy which was one of his conquering charms, "and when I saw your light still burning and your desk still covered with papers I knew you could not be far away and so I came on here."

I was strangely glad to see him. There was beginning to steal over me a vague uneasiness which threatened, as it had often done before, to blot out the light. Teüfelsdröckh was already whispering in my ear that underneath the beauty and midnight calm of Weissnichtwo was always, somewhere, "wretchedness cowering into its truckle bed." I did not want to listen, and when I heard his voice I felt suddenly as I used to do when as a child after puzzling and puzzling over a sum that would not come right, and all the world seemed to be nothing but toil, a well-loved teacher would come and ask me what the trouble was and, taking the pencil from me, settle down to work it out.

We did not speak for a moment, and then the Visitor turned to me suddenly with his question, Had I ever heard the story of the City of Two Times Two?

City of Two Times Two

"Why, no," I replied with a smile, suspecting a joke, but fired with sudden interest nevertheless, "but I should like to. Is it a fairy-story?"

The Visitor laughed. "No," he said, "it is not a fairy-story, but a very true story."

And then, after a moment—

"It happened this way. Many years ago there was a great city known throughout all the country round about as the City of Two Times Two. Into this city merchants and countrymen from far and near brought their merchandise and the fruits of their fields, and there was much buying and selling in its streets and market places. It was, as you may imagine, a very wealthy city, and being greatly favoured in the matter of situation there would seem to be no limit to the extent to which it might grow and prosper.

"From the very first, however, from the time long before any of the inhabitants, or any of their fathers or grandfathers, could remember this city had laboured under a difficulty, a difficulty the final dissipation of which no man had been able to achieve. Every man in the city would be confronted with this difficulty sooner or later, some of them much more often than others; while every man, without a single exception, no matter how prosperous or wealthy he might be, was overcome by it in the end and dropped from the life of the city.

"The difficulty lay in their process of reckoning. There were certain well known and carefully observed and carefully taught rules of reckoning, and for the most part those rules achieved satisfactory results; at any rate, the results—whether the rules were really responsible for them or not—were declared to be the best that could be obtained.

"Nevertheless, these problems could occasion great trouble and unhappiness. Research was constantly being made for new and more effective ways of meeting the trouble. Great schools had grown up through the years wherein men called 'adjusters' were fitted for the task of combating the difficulty, and everyone in his secret heart hoped that some day the final solution would be found and that the difficulty would disappear for ever.

"No man knew where it came from. Some

City of Two Times Two

people always seemed to be meeting it in some form or another, but curiously enough they were often the people who were the last to be overcome and to be dropped from the life of the city. Whereas someone who had never had it to meet, but had always been notorious among his friends for the ease with which he made his reckonings would be one day stricken down in his tracks, and before his friends could take their breath would have been dropped from the life of the city, sometimes even before an adjuster could reach his place of business.

"Well, it chanced on a day that a very prosperous citizen of that city was suddenly confronted with this difficulty in a very aggravated form. He summoned the best adjusters to his aid, and they later on summoned others. At first they thought they might be able to solve his problem for him, indeed were sure that they could, and spoke about it with much confidence. But later on, as their efforts proved unsuccessful, they began to be discouraged and, later on still, lost all hope, and told the citizen that it was only a matter of time before he would be dropped from the life of the city.

"It was often the case that when a verdict like this was rendered by the adjusters, the citizen concerning whose estate such judgment was given would withdraw from the city and betake himself to the country, very often to the part of the country where he was born, vainly hoping that amid the quiet of hill or valley he might find what the adjusters could not. This is just what the citizen I am telling you about did. He went to the little village where he was born, and there laboured over his papers, hoping to find a solution but growing more tired and despondent every day.

"Well, it happened one evening, feeling more than usually cast down, he went out for a walk among the hills, climbing higher and travelling farther than he had ever done before.

"And so it came about that as he reached the top of a certain hill, and looked down into the valley on the other side, he saw sitting on a rock just below him a Shepherd boy passing some sheep into a fold.

City of Two Times Two

"Almost mechanically the Stranger—for so he had called himself when he came to the village—began to count the sheep, wondering if he could reckon them rightly. They finished their count together and the Stranger called to the Shepherd boy.

" 'Son, tell me, how many do you reckon?'

"The boy looked round with a happy smile:

" 'Why, Master, one hundred and fifty-four—just right.'

"Now the Stranger had reckoned the number at one hundred and fifty. At first he was sick at heart because the matter seemed to show him, once again, how he could not reckon rightly even in this so small a thing. Next moment, however, he was ready to dispute the matter. Was he indeed to stand corrected by a Shepherd boy? He would talk with him. And so he did. He talked with him for long, reasoning this way and that, unfolding to the lad all the learning of the great City of Two Times Two: trying to make him see that twice two, instead of being four, as the boy ignorantly declared it to be, was indeed—as they had for so long known in the city—five.

The Visitor

"But the Shepherd boy only laughed.

" 'Why, as to that, Sir,' he said, 'I know nothing, but I do know that when two sheep pass under my rod and then another two that I have four sheep in the fold.'

"But the Stranger would have none of it. 'What have sheep got to do with it?' he said. 'Am I a shepherd that I should reckon that way?' And, being greatly angered, he strode away.

"He had not gone far, however, before something seemed to come to him. He turned and came quickly towards the Shepherd boy, pulling a bundle of paper from his bosom as he did so.

" 'Here,' he said, as he came up with him, thrusting the papers into his hands, 'here, since you know so much, try your hand at these.'

"The Shepherd boy took them. He began at the beginning and, slowly at first, but ever gaining in confidence, went through them all right to the end. Wherever he found twice two reckoned as five he reckoned it as four. The Stranger sat by his side, at first in unbelief, holding him in derision, later on in silence, and later on still as he saw all his difficulties being cleared away and new life held out to him, with tears of gratitude."

The Visitor stopped speaking and all around the great silence seemed more silent than ever. Even the tree-toad no longer uttered his voice. The full moon had mounted high into the heavens, and, all silver now where before it had been gold, was racing amid the clouds high up above the tree-tops. After a moment or two the Visitor spoke again.

"Some years later I was passing through the City of Two Times Two on a journey and on entering I found the whole city in an uproar. I asked one who stood by what it meant. After remarking that I must indeed be a stranger if I did not know, he told me concerning the matter, how some years before a Shepherd boy had come into the city from the hills accompanied by a former citizen of high estate who had been dropped from the life of the city but was now returned—in itself an unprecedented thing—to claim his own again. This citizen, he told me, declared that he had been healed of his difficulty

The Visitor

by the Shepherd boy and he begged all his fellow-citizens to hear the lad. Many did hear him, it seems, but the authorities, led by the adjusters, arrayed themselves against him and only a short time before my arrival the worthy citizen had been slain and now to-day the Shepherd was to be put to death also.

"At that moment," the Visitor continued, "I looked up and saw them coming towards me, a great crowd of men and women and children. They were shouting and throwing dust in the air, and seeking to beat with staves a Shepherd who was being led by a guard of soldiers through the streets towards the gates of the city. And as they went, time and again, the crowd cried out, 'Certainly he is worthy of death.' And so they took him without the gates of the city, to a desert place, and there they stoned him until he died." There was another silence. The scene at our feet seemed to grow in splendour and peace as the reassurance of the Shepherd boy, with his eyes only on the Truth, insensibly encompassed me round about.

"I think," said the Visitor after a little while,

City of Two Times Two

"that is the answer, is it not? It is beautiful because for the moment mortal man, the only strife-maker, is asleep and we are thus better able to see things as they really are—to see twice two as four. Mortal man is asleep," he went on as if speaking to himself, "and when mortal man is asleep, where is the sin and the murder and all the unkindness?"

Another silence and then this:

"And so, no matter how great the storm, the perplexity of doubt and bafflement may seem to be, to those who understand, as did the Shepherd boy, there will always be—a great calm. The more faithfully we know this and abide in it, the more surely will those who cry to us, being in jeopardy, learn the power of our—'Peace, be still!'"

CHAPTER SEVEN

What Happened to John's Wife

THE next time I saw the Visitor—it was the last time I ever saw him—I was destined to pass through in his company one of those strange experiences which the world would account miraculous, but which, with the Visitor, seemed not only natural but inevitable.

It was late at night, in the autumn of the year. The day had been a warm one, but darkness had fallen crisp and clear, with a radiant hunter's-moon mounting up into the high heaven, transforming the mists of the valley into snowfields and blotting out the stars.

The light in the upper windows of the woodsman's cottage had gone out, and there was just stealing over me that much treasured sense of being the only one awake, when a knock came to my door followed immediately by a slow lifting of the latch, and, next moment, the Visitor was standing in the doorway silhouetted against the moonlight.

John's Wife

"I am on my way," he said, "to see John's wife. I had a message a little while ago to say that a little son had been born to her, but that she was very sick and that the doctor feared she could not live and she was asking for me. So I am going, of course. I wondered as I passed and saw your lamp still burning whether you would like to come with me. She would like to see you and so would John. Will you come?"

"Yes, indeed," I answered, "I can be with you almost immediately. Come in and warm yourself while I get into my shoes and that old leather coat of mine."

As I laced my shoes I glanced at him from time to time. He stood looking into the fire. There was a strange expression on his face— I do not know how to describe it—a look of weariness and yet of strength and confidence and an infinite practical compassion.

A few moments later we were on the road down the hill, our feet falling silently on the carpet of pine needles.

It had all happened so suddenly I had hardly had time to think, but now my mind was filled

The Visitor

with rebellion. Only a few days before, I had stepped in to see John's wife. I had known her since she was a child, watched her grow up and seen her happily married. I had found her sitting in the little porch in the sunlight sewing, with a look of unutterable joy in her eyes. She had spoken simply, with the confidence of a child in an old friend, about the baby that was coming; how John hoped it would be a boy, and how she hoped it would be a boy if John hoped it would, but that if it was a little girl how they would both love her more than anything else in the world, and how wonderful it all was, and how good God was, and how good I was, and how good everybody was.

And now look what had happened. Just as the cup of happiness was raised to her lips it had been dashed to the ground. It was outrageous—past belief. The child had asked for bread and had not only been given a stone, but had been thrown to the ground and kicked in the face. "I can't believe in such a God," I muttered to myself as I buttoned the collar of my coat impatiently and quickened my pace.

John's Wife

"You should not," said the Visitor, laying a hand gently on my shoulder. "Nobody should. The worship of such a God is of course mere devil worship. But there is in reality no such God. Our God is of purer eyes than to behold evil and cannot look upon iniquity. We can know that and be sure of it—and prove it."

"Then what do you make of this wretched tragedy which is going to be enacted before our very eyes?"

"I am going to see it as God sees it," he replied simply, "and you are going to help me. But see, here is someone coming from the cottage."

A man and a woman were approaching us. There was a strange air of dejection about them, and, as they came nearer, I noticed that the woman was crying bitterly, the man walking beside her with that stolid wretchedness with which a man so often meets sorrow. It was Michael, the teamster, and his wife. We knew them well. He was a great friend of John's and she had gone to school with John's wife.

As soon as the woman saw us she ran eagerly towards the Visitor.

The Visitor

"Oh, sir," she cried, through her tears, "why weren't you here? I know if you had been here Robin would not have died. Yes, sir, she's dead," she replied in answer to my hurried question, "died about half an hour ago, crying for her baby and kind of feeling round for John, the poor lamb."

They turned and walked back with us. The Visitor said nothing, but looked from one to another with an expression of tenderness which instantly checked a surge of rebellion just then threatening to overwhelm me. For the first time since I had known him I saw tears coursing slowly down his face. It seemed a long time before anyone spoke again, and then as we reached the garden gate the Visitor said simply:

"She is not really dead, Michael, not really, Mary. She is only asleep."

Words of instant protest sprang to the man's lips. He knew she was dead. The doctor had said she was dead, and had left a good half hour ago. Mary, too, joined him in assurance. But the Visitor, with a kindly gesture, passed on up the little iris-lined pathway into the house.

John's Wife

The living-room seemed to be full of people; the women weeping silently, the men standing round afraid to meet each other's eyes, twisting their hats in their hands, waiting for the women to have done and come away.

"Oh, sir," cried one little woman, rushing towards him as he entered, "she's gone. She that was always that kind and sunny like."

"She is still kind and sunny," said the Visitor, "she is not dead."

A moment's tense silence followed this statement. And then one woman, who had been speaking as the Visitor entered, spoke again:

"There is no use saying that, sir," she said. "Robin Lovejoy is dead. She died for her sins and John Lovejoy lost her for his sins, and unless he sees that and repents, unless we all see that and repent, God will do to us what he has done to John's wife and more also."

As she finished, the Visitor opened his lips as if to speak, and then closed them again. With a motion of the hands inexpressibly eloquent he signified that there was nothing to be said, and that he would be alone. So they filed out, one by one, with murmured words of leave-taking; the woman who had last spoken of all without looking at him.

The next moment we were in Robin's room.

She lay with her hands crossed upon her breast, her hair like a golden aureole framing her face, and spreading itself out on the pillows on either side. By the bedside knelt John, his face buried in the coverlet, his arms stretched out across the tiny mound which marked the feet of the dead girl.

He did not move as we entered, and the Visitor went and stood beside him. The uncertain flame of a single candle by the bedside was the only source of light. John was in the shadow, but the light which in its passage illumined gently Robin's still features, shone full on the face of the Visitor.

I looked at him with a strange eagerness and expectancy. What was he going to do? And why was it that as I watched him I found myself repeating over and over and over again, "The wind bloweth where it listeth, and thou hearest the sound thereof, but canst not tell whence

John's Wife

it cometh and whither it goeth; so is everyone that is born of the Spirit"?

At last he spoke, very slowly and haltingly at first, but gathering a great confidence as he went on as though addressing a real presence. As far as I can recall it, this is what he said:

"There is no death. O Father, give it to me at this moment to see this most clearly. For Thou art Life, Thou art *That Which Is*, and that which is is all there is. So all there is is Life, and death has no dominion. O Father, hitherto we have seen through a glass darkly, but now we are beginning to see face to face, and as we see more clearly we see more surely that everything unlike Thee can be no part of that which is, and so must be that which is not—a lie, a liar and the father of it. O Father, the world is full of these lies, weary and heavy-laden men and women, sick and sinful, sorry, poor, wretched and dying; but right in the place where each one of these mistakes appears to be, these twice-two-is-fives, over which like tired children before our much-rubbed slates we are weeping wretchedly, right there is the forever fact of the right answer—Man, perfect as his Father in Heaven is perfect—perfect as *That Which Is* is perfect. Open our eyes that we may see."

There was a long pause during which the only sound was the low murmur of the breeze through the pines, and then the Visitor spoke again:

"This child," he said, "is not dead. Before Abraham was she is, and all that the Father hath is hers. 'He that believeth on me, though he were dead yet shall he live, and he that liveth and believeth on me shall never die.' "

Another pause and then:

"Lord, I believe. I do not care how much my poor blind humanity may scoff at me; how much it may try to overwhelm me out of the mouth of many witnesses; how much it may flaunt before me the seemingly so real sorrows of the world, its wars, its pestilences, its shameless cruelty, its sin, its sickness, its death and worse than death. I take my stand where you bid me stand and I say that my God is of purer eyes than to behold evil and cannot look upon iniquity. And I stand and wait and wait—and *know*. . . . She is not dead but sleepeth. Robin, I say unto thee, awake."

John's Wife

And Robin awoke. And, shaking her hair back from her shoulders, her eyes sought the face of the Visitor.

"Oh, sir," she cried, "I knew it would be you. Where is John?"

As I opened the door for us to pass out, I looked back. Robin was sitting up in bed clasping to her breast a little bundle hastily brought in, in awestricken wonder, by a woman from the adjoining room. Her face was upturned. Her right hand passed backwards and forwards through John's hair as he wept silently, his face buried in her lap.

And so it came about that as I looked round for him, he was gone, and I was alone. I felt strangely forsaken, for somehow I knew that I should never see him again as I had seen him in times past.

Why had he gone? He had carried me up on to the topmost peak of the mount of transfiguration, and when I would, there, have built me a tabernacle, counting to dwell therein thenceforward and be at peace, he had vanished away. When I called, there was no voice nor any that answered.

As I waited with eyes cast down, being much at a loss, lo, suddenly, I heard a voice behind me, very near, saying, "Here is the path, walk ye in it."

And, looking up, I beheld a path leading down the hillside into a valley below through which there ran a great river. From the other side of this river there came the sound of many voices, and they cried saying, "Come over and help us!"

As I listened, behold the cry became exceeding loud and full of much sorrow, "Come over and help us!"

And when I would yet have waited, behold the voice behind me came again saying, "Lo, the kingdoms of this world are become the kingdom of our God and of His Christ. Yet there be many whose eyes are still holden and whose ears are shut. And how shall they call on Him in whom they have not believed? And how shall they believe in Him of whom they have not heard? And how shall they hear without a preacher? And how shall they preach, except they be sent? Go over and help them, and the things thou hast heard in secret, proclaim openly. And lo, as thou goest, be not sorrowful but rejoicing, as it is written, 'How beautiful on the mountains are the feet of them that preach the gospel of peace, and bring glad tidings of good things.' "

THE GARDEN OF THE BELOVED
Robert Way

The beautifully written and original story of a rich young man who seeks to learn the art of loving from a humble gardener who tends the Garden of the Beloved.

'It is a subject on which so much has been written before. Yet Robert Way has, I am sure, caught with a few words the essential truth with an insight akin to the great classical works on the subject.'

Delia Smith

' . . . A book of genius, akin to Kahil Gibran's THE PROPHET, which is likely to become a classic. It's fascinating, humbling and inspiring.'

FK Bulletin

'It is short . . . it is simple, and it is beautifully written. In my opinion it is superb—and I do not say that lightly.'

East Anglian Daily Times

'I found it a book of sheer delight . . . It was pure pleasure to read, and with its timeless style I have no doubt that it will become a worldwide classic.'

David Watson

'Easy to read, simple and profound.'

The Old Lady of Threadneedle Street

'A really delightful book.'

Colin Cowdrey

THE WISDOM OF THE DESERT
Thomas Merton

The ancient hermits were holy men. They rejected the bogus conformity of the world and sought true freedom in the deserts of Egypt and Palestine. They had much in common with Zen Buddhist monks and Indian yogis. Many came to them for advice and their sayings were remembered, passed on and written down.

Their wisdom was simple, practical and timeless.

'I loved the Wisdom of the Desert but to ask me for a few words of commendation on the sayings of the elders is like a request to dance in front of Dame Margot or sing to Caruso in his bath.'

Auberon Waugh

'Merton believed as I do, that "we need to learn from these men of the Fourth Century".'

Kenneth Leech

'A remarkable collection. Merton is always compulsively readable.'

The Universe

'In the age of affluence the value of the lives of holy men can still be recognized.'

The Times

'We cannot all retire to the desert in solitude to weave baskets and pray but from these monks we can learn something of the basic realities of the interior life which are valid for all ages.'

Sean Fagan SM

'Every time we return to these timeless sayings we are sure to meet a pearl.'

Frederick Hockey OSB

'His prose is a delight to read.'

The Evangelical Quarterly

'Full of marvellous things.'

BBC Radio Medway

'Superb material for contemplating, for daily reflection and thoughts wherever we are. A most timely, gentle book.'

World Faiths

' . . . selective in his choice of the sayings so that the 150 of this collection are pearls.'

Church Scene (Australia)

'A delightful book full of humour as well as wisdom.'

The Franciscan
